Love That Puppy!

The Story of a Boy
Who Wanted to Be a Dog

by Jeff Jarka

Henry Holt and Company
New York

Peter was an ordinary boy at first.

Then, one day, Peter decided to become a dog.

Not everyone thought this was a good idea.

But Peter was happy.

Peter was good at being a puppy. He knew how to sit up.

And he knew how to beg.

Like all dogs, Peter loved to go for long rides . . .

. . . and sleep at his masters' feet.

He liked to play fetch with his dad.

He liked to eat from his favorite dish.

He learned to perform simple tricks.

And he had excellent hearing.

Peter practiced his bark so that
he could be the best guard dog ever.

But while Peter was good at being a dog,
he was not always a good dog.

He chased cars.

His schoolwork was suffering.

He developed an unhealthy interest in the mail . . .

. . . and the mailman.

Then, one day . . .

Peter's parents had had enough.
They asked him to stop being a dog.
This made Peter very sad.

HOOooooooOWL

That night Peter thought about what they said.
Maybe he should be a boy again,
like everyone wanted.

The next morning Peter was no longer a dog.
Peter was an ordinary boy again.

Everyone was very happy.

For Theresa

Henry Holt and Company, LLC
Publishers since 1866
175 Fifth Avenue
New York, New York 10010
www.HenryHoltKids.com

Henry Holt® is a registered trademark of Henry Holt and Company, LLC.
Copyright © 2009 by Jeff Jarka
All rights reserved.
Distributed in Canada by H. B. Fenn and Company Ltd.

Library of Congress Cataloging-in-Publication Data
Jarka, Jeff.
Love that puppy! : the story of a boy who wanted to be a dog / Jeff Jarka.—1st ed.
p.   cm.
Summary: When his parents want him to change back into a human boy,
Peter the dog comes up with a novel solution.
ISBN-13: 978-0-8050-8741-3
ISBN-10: 0-8050-8741-9
[1. Dogs—Fiction. 2. Human-animal relationships—Fiction.] I. Title.
PZ7.J285Lo 2009
[E]—dc22
2008018333
First Edition—2009
Printed in the United States of America on acid-free paper. ∞

1 3 5 7 9 10 8 6 4 2

The artist used Adobe® Photoshop® to create the illustrations for this book.